Stolen Dia

Elizabeth held her breath as Mr. Doyle walked away. Then she let out a loud sigh.

"Now he knows we know," Eva whispered, her eyes wide. "What should we do?"

"It's a race for the diamonds," Todd said with a grin.

Elizabeth noticed a clock nearby. "It's also a race against time," she reminded them. "We only have forty-five minutes to go."

"Oh, no!" Ellen wailed. "Where should we start?"

"We can't let Mr. Doyle get the diamonds," Jessica said. "I think we should follow him. That way, if he finds them, we'll be there to stop him."

Elizabeth nodded. "OK. He just got on the up escalator."

"He's going back to the scene of the crime!" Todd said.

"Yikes!" Amy said. "Let's go!"

Bantam Books in the
SWEET VALLEY KIDS series

SWEET VALLEY KIDS
SUPER SNOOPER #6

THE CASE OF THE MILLION–DOLLAR DIAMONDS

Written by
Molly Mia Stewart

Created by
FRANCINE PASCAL

Illustrated by
Ying-Hwa Hu

A BANTAM SKYLARK BOOK
NEW YORK • TORONTO • LONDON • SYDNEY • AUCKLAND

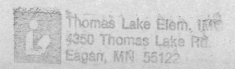

RL 2, 005-008

THE CASE OF THE MILLION-DOLLAR DIAMONDS
A Bantam Skylark Book / December 1993

*Sweet Valley High® and Sweet Valley Kids are
trademarks of Francine Pascal*

Conceived by Francine Pascal

*Produced by Daniel Weiss Associates, Inc.
33 West 17th Street
New York, NY 10011*

Cover art by Susan Tang

*Skylark Books is a registered trademark of Bantam Books, a
division of Bantam Doubleday Dell Publishing Group, Inc.
Registered in U.S. Patent and Trademark Office and elsewhere.*

ISBN: 0-553-48115-0

Published simultaneously in the United States and Canada

*Bantam Books are published by Bantam Books, a division of Bantam
Doubleday Dell Publishing Group, Inc. Its trademark, consisting of the
words "Bantam Books" and the portrayal of a rooster, is Registered in
U.S. Patent and Trademark Office and in other countries. Marca
Registrada. Bantam Books, 1540 Broadway, New York, New York 10036.*

PRINTED IN THE UNITED STATES OF AMERICA

CWO   0 9 8 7 6 5 4 3 2 1

To Olivia Grace Vaccaro

CHAPTER 1

A Christmas Wish

Elizabeth Wakefield stamped her feet and hugged her arms around herself. "Brrr! It's c-c-cold up here in the North P-p-pole!" she said, her teeth chattering.

"I'm f-freezing," her twin sister, Jessica, agreed.

They looked at the snow and icicles hanging from Santa's Village and laughed. The snow and icicles were fake. Living in Sweet Valley, California, meant it was warm all year, even at Christmas. The North Pole display at the mall was the closest they usually got to snow and ice. At the moment, they were waiting to get their pictures taken on Santa's lap.

"I'll tell you how you can get a taste of something cold," their father said with a smile. "Who wants ice cream?"

"Me!" Elizabeth and Jessica both shouted.

"And how about your friends?" Mr. Wakefield asked.

Standing on line with them were Elizabeth's and Jessica's best friends from their second-grade class. Lila Fowler, Ellen Riteman, Eva Simpson, Amy Sutton, Todd Wilkins, and Winston Egbert were lined up like toy soldiers, waiting their turns. Each of them said, "Yes, please" to ice cream.

"This will be the eighth year in a row I get my picture taken on Santa's lap,"

Lila bragged as Mr. Wakefield left to buy the ice cream.

"How can that be?" Todd asked. "You're only seven."

Lila smiled a know-it-all smile. "Because my mother came while she was pregnant, that's how."

"Our mom said once that she asked Santa to bring her twins," Jessica said as the line inched closer to Santa Claus. "And he did!"

Elizabeth and Jessica were not only twins, they were *identical* twins. They looked as similar as two snowflakes. Both girls had blue-green eyes and long blond hair with bangs. It was hard to tell them apart. Even their friends often had to check the name bracelets each twin wore, to make sure they were speaking to the right person.

And just as snowflakes look identical

but are really all different, Elizabeth and Jessica were different in important ways, too. Jessica liked playing with dolls and pretending to be a ballerina. On the other hand, Elizabeth enjoyed reading and playing soccer. She did her homework right away, while Jessica waited until the last moment. And even when they picked matching outfits, Elizabeth chose hers in blue or green, and Jessica insisted on pink or purple.

Those differences didn't matter, however. They shared a bedroom, they shared clothes and toys, and they shared secrets that nobody else knew. They were best friends.

"Here's ice cream for everyone," Mr. Wakefield said when he returned. He asked Jessica and Elizabeth to hand out Popsicles to their friends.

"We're just like Santa's helpers," Elizabeth said, giggling. She pointed to some children dressed as elves, who were helping in the Santa's Village display. "Doesn't that look like fun?"

"I hope we have something fun to do during school vacation," Ellen said, licking her Popsicle carefully.

"You know what would be the best?" Winston said. He lowered his voice and glanced around. "If we had another mystery to solve. We're the Snoopers Club, after all."

Already the Snoopers had solved some exciting mysteries. They'd caught a thief at school, dug for gold treasure at the beach and found a valuable charm bracelet, unmasked the identity of the "ghost" haunting Camp San Benito, and solved many more cases. The thought of a new case made Elizabeth's heart speed up.

"That would be so cool," she agreed. "Maybe it'll be a mystery at the mall."

Lila shook her head. "Look around," she said grumpily.

Elizabeth and the others did as Lila said. Around them holiday shoppers jostled cheerfully as they browsed through the mall. Christmas carols played over the loudspeakers, and someone nearby was ringing a bell. The smell of peppermint filled the air.

"So?" Amy asked Lila as the Snoopers all took a step closer to the head of the line. "What do you want us to see?"

"That this place is ordinary," Lila explained in a bored voice. "We're not going to find a mystery here."

Elizabeth frowned. "We might. You have to be positive."

Suddenly she realized she was at the head of the line.

"Go on!" Jessica said, nudging Elizabeth in the back.

Elizabeth walked toward Santa Claus. She knew he was only a normal person pretending to be someone else, but she was excited anyway.

"Do you have the Christmas spirit, little girl?" Santa said in a cheerful voice.

"I sure do," Elizabeth answered. She smiled as she made herself comfortable on his lap.

"And do you have a special wish?" he asked.

Elizabeth closed her eyes, took a deep breath, and nodded.

"I wish . . . I wish for a mystery!"

CHAPTER 2

Diamonds and Ice

"And a pink bicycle and a pony and a guitar," Jessica read from her wish list. "And—"

"I think I can take it from there," Santa Claus interrupted, chuckling. "Now, smile for the camera."

Jessica faced the camera. "Cheese!" she said, and then jumped down from Santa's lap.

"Now," Mr. Wakefield said to the Snoopers still standing on line. "I have a quick errand to do, but I'll be back before you can say Kriss Kringle, OK?"

"Sure, Mr. Wakefield," Todd replied. "We'll stay right here."

"Can we go with you, Dad?" Elizabeth asked.

Mr. Wakefield nodded, and Jessica and Elizabeth skipped along beside him through the crowded aisles. "I want to visit one of my clients," he said. Mr. Wakefield was a lawyer. "Mr. Fox has a jewelry store here in the mall. I might just find something for Mom."

Jessica twirled around. "How about a diamond tiara!" she suggested hopefully.

"So you can wear it for dress-up?" Elizabeth teased.

"I wasn't going to spend more than three or four million dollars," their father joked as they went up the escalator. "So let's try to keep it simple."

Giggling, Jessica followed her father

and Elizabeth into a fancy jewelry store. There was a deep, soft carpet on the floor, and beautiful violin music came from hidden speakers.

"Well, hello!" cried out a tall, thin man with glasses. "Happy holidays, Mr. Wakefield." He made his way over after finishing up with a couple who left the shop. "And who are these two gorgeous young ladies?" Mr. Fox asked.

"These are my special shopping advisers," Mr. Wakefield said, shaking Mr. Fox's hand. "Elizabeth and Jessica."

Jessica smiled and bent over to look in a display case. She pressed her nose against the glass. The case was filled with gold necklaces, diamond and ruby and emerald pendants, sparkling rings and watches.

"How about these blue earrings, Dad?" Jessica said, looking in another case.

"They're sapphires," Mr. Fox explained. "Aren't they beautiful?"

"Beautiful, and way, *way* out of my price range," Mr. Wakefield said, shaking his head.

"Let me show you a few less-expensive things," Mr. Fox said kindly as he put a red velvet mat on the counter. "Not everything costs an arm and a leg."

Jessica and Elizabeth looked around the shop and went over to a countertop display of crystal vases and silver picture frames. Everything gleamed in the light.

"I've never seen so much fancy stuff." Elizabeth whispered. "I'm afraid to touch anything."

"Jessica, Elizabeth," Mr. Fox called. "Would you like to see something very special?"

Jessica and Elizabeth both nodded. "Sure," they said as they hurried back to the counter where their father and Mr. Fox were standing. Mr. Wakefield was looking at a gold bracelet.

Mr. Fox unlocked a cabinet in the wall, opened a door, and then twirled a combination lock. "Wow! It's a safe!" Elizabeth gasped.

"That's right," Mr. Fox said as he took out a black velvet pouch.

The bell to the store rang as new customers came in. Jessica turned and saw two men in suits and ties go toward a glass case. One of the men was young, with neatly cut brown hair; the other was older, with curly white hair. Both looked very distinguished. Jessica wondered if they were going to buy lots of gifts.

"Jess," Elizabeth said, nudging her. "Pay attention. You're going to miss the surprise."

Jessica turned back. "Is this a secret?"

she whispered, not wanting the new-comers to hear.

"Sure. Let's just say it's a private viewing," Mr. Fox said. He untied the pouch and carefully poured a cluster of five precious gems onto a velvet mat. A lamp shone on them, making flashes of light shoot out in all directions.

Jessica and Elizabeth stared in astonishment. "Diamonds!" Elizabeth said, barely breathing. "Look how they sparkle!"

"They almost look like ice!" Jessica said.

Mr. Wakefield nodded. "Some people call diamonds ice. You can see why. Thanks a lot for letting us see them, Mr. Fox."

"My pleasure," the jeweler said proudly, putting them into the pouch again.

Jessica glanced over her shoulder.

The two businessmen were looking at a display of gold bracelets, but from time to time they looked at Mr. Fox.

"Psst," Jessica whispered to her sister. "Maybe those two men are going to rob the store."

Elizabeth's eyebrows went up in surprise. "No way. They don't look like robbers to me."

"I know," Jessica said with a sigh. "I was just hoping they would. Then we'd have a case."

"Time to go," Mr. Wakefield announced. "I'm not going to buy anything just yet. Thanks for your help, Mr. Fox." He shook the jeweler's hand. "Now we'd better get back to your friends."

CHAPTER 3

The Big Alarm

Elizabeth pretended to be skiing as they went down the escalator, bending her knees and holding her fists out in front of her. "I can see Eva and the others," she said. "It looks like they're all done."

"Weren't you kids going to look for a present for your teacher?" Mr. Wakefield asked.

"Yes," Jessica replied. "But we can't decide what to get."

They joined their friends near Santa's Village, by a sign that said, No Penguins Beyond This Point. Elizabeth giggled as she read it. The loudspeakers were blaring out "Jingle Bells."

"I vote we get Mrs. Otis a hat with a feather in it," Winston announced. "Like Robin Hood's."

Amy and Eva both laughed, and Todd pretended he was shooting an arrow into the tall ceiling of the mall. From a distance they heard Santa laughing, "Ho, ho, ho!"

"That is the dumbest idea, Win," Lila complained. "No teacher wants to look like Robin Hood."

"What do *you* want to get her?" Winston asked, raising his voice over the jingling bells. "Some chalk?"

"How about some of the diamonds we just saw?" Jessica said.

Her eyes twinkled. "They must have been worth about a million dollars."

"You're kidding!" Ellen's eyes widened.

Elizabeth shook her head. "No, we really saw—"

At that moment a deafening bell clanged through the mall. For an instant Elizabeth thought it was part of "Jingle Bells." But then—

"That's an alarm!" Mr. Wakefield shouted.

The Snoopers spun around at the sound of voices yelling on the upper level. All around them, shoppers were bumping into each other and asking what was happening. Elizabeth and Jessica and the others stood on tiptoe to see better.

"My diamonds!" came a shout. "They stole my diamonds!"

Elizabeth grabbed Jessica's hand. On the second level of the mall, they saw a crowd of men running for the escalator.

Mr. Fox and several security guards were bringing up the rear. The alarm was still clanging so loudly that Elizabeth could hardly hear herself think. She did hear several people shout "Fire!" and begin to scream.

"Stop them!" Mr. Fox was yelling.

The runners tore down the escalator, bumping into shoppers as they went. Packages went flying, and someone's candy cane sailed through the air and landed on a bald man's head.

"Look out!"

"Stop them!"

"Hey! Watch it!"

At the front of the pack, a brown-haired man in a business suit crashed through a picket fence into Santa's Village. He knocked over two reindeer and shoved an elf out of the way. The guards and Mr. Fox and several more men tore after him, yelling and waving their arms.

"They're coming this way!" Ellen screamed.

Elizabeth and Jessica and the other Snoopers backed into the penguin sign as the man burst out of Santa's Village and headed right for them. Ellen screamed again. Then Winston stuck his foot out, and the man tripped over it, stumbling headfirst into a Christmas tree. A security guard dove after him.

"Gotcha!" came a shout of triumph from within the tinseled branches.

CHAPTER 4

The Brown-Haired Man

"Let go of me!" an angry voice roared. "Let me go!"

The Christmas-tree branches rustled vigorously, and the security guard backed out, pulling the man in a suit with him.

"How dare you!" the man shouted. He yanked a strand of tinsel from his eyebrow.

Jessica clutched Elizabeth's arm. "That's one of the men!" she said. "The men I was hoping would rob Mr. Fox. And they did!"

"Where are the diamonds?" the security guard demanded.

"I don't know what you're talking about," the man said. "Diamonds? What diamonds?"

Mr. Fox and the others skidded to a halt. "Where are they?" Mr. Fox said, panting. "What did you do with my diamonds?"

The captured businessman scowled fiercely as the security guard began to search his pockets. "I didn't take anything," he declared. "Like I said, I don't have your stupid diamonds."

"Maybe he gave them to his friend," Jessica suggested.

"Who are you talking about?" Mr. Wakefield asked.

Jessica pointed at the man. "I saw him and another man when we were in Mr. Fox's store," she explained. "They were watching Mr. Fox show us the diamonds."

She craned her neck to look around the mall, but there was no sign of the older businessman. Dozens of curious shoppers with their arms full of packages crowded around to watch what was happening.

"What did the other man look like?" Todd whispered.

"He had curly white hair and a black tie with red stripes," Jessica said. "But I don't see him."

Mr. Fox grabbed the captive's briefcase. "Open it up!" he ordered.

"I will," the man said huffily, snapping open the locks. "But only to prove I have nothing to hide. I didn't take your diamonds."

"Then why did you run?" Elizabeth spoke up loudly.

"Huh?" The man whirled around, then sneered when he saw Elizabeth was a kid. "Mind your own business."

"Why *did* you run?" the security guard asked.

"Because six angry men were chasing me!" the businessman shouted, his face turning red. "I thought I was going to be attacked. Which is just what happened."

Mr. Fox was frantically searching the man's briefcase, but there wasn't a trace of the diamonds. He handed back the case with a worried sigh and shook his head. "What could have happened?"

"I demand that you release me," the businessman warned."Or else I'll have you charged with assault and kidnapping!"

The security guards shrugged their shoulders. "We really can't hold him," one of them explained to Mr. Fox.

"There's nothing to show he stole your diamonds."

"But . . . But . . ." Mr. Fox sputtered.

"Maybe you didn't take them," the guard said to the businessman. "But you'd better keep clear of this mall. I don't want to see your face here again."

"I'm going, I'm going," the man snapped. "I resent being treated in this shameful manner." He slammed his briefcase shut, straightened his tie, and strode away.

Mr. Fox took his glasses off and polished them nervously. "What am I going to do?" he groaned. "My business will be ruined if I don't get those diamonds back!"

"You should call the police," Mr. Wakefield said. "Tell them exactly what happened."

The crowd began to wander off. Mr. Fox and Mr. Wakefield sat down on a bench to discuss the situation, while Jessica and Elizabeth and the rest of the Snoopers gathered in a huddle next to the caved-in Christmas tree.

"I'm sure that man and his friend stole the diamonds," Jessica said.

"What makes you so sure?" Todd asked. "He doesn't look like a thief to me."

"I just know it," Jessica said. "He was in the jewelry store *and* he ran."

Elizabeth nodded. "I think he stole them, too."

Eva and Winston and Amy agreed, but the others weren't quite convinced.

"Look at it this way," Elizabeth said. "We wanted a mystery, and we've got one."

Lila wrinkled her nose and bent down to tie her shoelaces. "I think it's all a mistake," she said. "I don't think that man did anything wrong. I mean, there wasn't—" Suddenly she stopped talking and stared at the floor.

"Lila?" Ellen asked when Lila didn't move. "What's wrong?"

Very slowly Lila stood up and held out her hand. In the middle of her palm sat one sparkling diamond.

CHAPTER 5

The White-Haired Man

"**H**oly cow!"
"Look at that!"
"Wow!"

The Snoopers stared at the diamond in amazement. Elizabeth's stomach flip-flopped. "He must have dropped that one!" she whispered.

"But where are the others?" Amy wondered out loud. "He didn't have them with him. The guards searched him."

"But now we're sure he's guilty. We have to figure out what he did with the other four," Elizabeth said. She looked at everyone in the Snoopers Club. "We definitely have a mystery to solve."

Todd scratched his head. "Maybe Jessica is right. He must have given the diamonds to his friend."

"The man with curly white hair and the striped tie!" Jessica said.

Eva was staring at the escalator. Her eyes widened and her mouth dropped open. "Do you mean . . ." She gestured with her head. "Him?"

The Snoopers all looked up. Coming down the escalator was a well-dressed man with curly white hair, a black tie with red stripes, and a raincoat folded over one arm.

"Yes!" Jessica squeaked. She opened her mouth to shout.

"Wait," Elizabeth said, grabbing her sister's elbow.

The man was frowning, looking back

up at the second level of the mall. When he reached the bottom of the escalator, he stopped and looked slowly around, shaking his head.

"If he has the diamonds, why isn't he escaping as fast as he can?" Ellen asked.

"He looks confused," Elizabeth whispered as the man looked over his shoulder.

"Like he's looking for something," Winston added.

"And doesn't know where it is," Jessica said.

Elizabeth gulped. "The diamonds. He doesn't know where they are," she said breathlessly. "He doesn't know what his friend did with them."

Todd snapped his fingers. "That means we can find them before he does."

Lila closed her fingers over the diamond in her hand. "What do we do with this one?"

"Let's not tell anyone we found it," Jessica said quickly. "If we do, all the grown-ups will take over the case. But if we find the rest of the diamonds ourselves, we'll be heroes."

"But if we *don't* find them, we'll get into trouble for not telling what we found," Ellen said in a worried voice.

"Let's vote," Todd said. "Who says we keep it a secret?"

One by one Elizabeth, Jessica, Amy, Winston, Todd, and Lila raised their hands. Then Eva put her hand up, and finally, Ellen did, too.

"There's just one problem," Jessica said. "We can't solve any mystery with Dad around."

Elizabeth frowned. "We'll just ask if we can go to some stores without him," she said. "Come on, Jess. Everyone else, stay here."

Elizabeth and Jessica hurried over to the bench where Mr. Wakefield and Mr. Fox were sitting. Elizabeth wanted to tell Mr. Fox not to worry. She was sure the Snoopers could find his diamonds, but she knew they couldn't say anything.

"Dad?" Elizabeth said. "Can we all go to the bookstore without you?"

Mr. Wakefield looked startled. "Why?"

Jessica crossed her fingers behind her back. "We're looking for a surprise for you," she fibbed.

Their father looked at them for a moment. He seemed doubtful.

"Please, Dad?" Elizabeth begged. "We need a little bit of time to shop alone."

At last he nodded. "OK. I'll give you one hour. See that clock over Santa's Village? I'll wait for you there one hour from now. Don't be a second late."

"We won't, Dad. We promise," Jessica said.

Elizabeth glanced at the clock. It read one minute before three. They had until four o'clock.

"One hour," Mr. Wakefield repeated.

Elizabeth and Jessica turned around. "We'll be back!" Elizabeth called as they began to run.

CHAPTER 6

Mr. Doyle

"We need a plan," Jessica announced as soon as she and Elizabeth joined the other Snoopers again. She glanced over at the white-haired man. He was examining a mall directory.

"But what do we do first?" Amy asked. "How are we going to find the diamonds while that thief is looking for them, too? He'll see us."

"I know what we should do," Lila said with a sneaky grin. "Eliminate the competition."

"You mean, get rid of him?" Todd asked.

"If I had a stun gun, I'd get him," Winston said, whipping out an imaginary gun from an imaginary holster. He aimed it at the suspect. "Zzzzap! Dreamland, mister!"

Lila rolled her eyes. "Oh, cut it out!"

"All we really have to do is tell the security guards he's one of the robbers," Elizabeth pointed out. "Then they'll kick him out of the mall."

"Right," Jessica agreed confidently. "Let's go."

Together they marched over to a security guard who was strolling past Santa's Village.

"Excuse me, sir," Elizabeth began in a polite voice. The guard smiled at them, and Elizabeth continued. "The man who took the diamonds is over there," she said.

The guard's smile vanished. "Where?" he asked.

Jessica pointed. "That man there with the curly white hair. I saw him and the other man in the jewelry store."

"Are you sure?" the guard asked, beginning to walk toward the suspect.

"Positive," Jessica said with a nod. "Cross my heart."

The Snoopers followed behind the security guard as he approached the white-haired man. Jessica could hardly stop smiling.

"This was so easy!" she whispered to Lila. Winston looked over and gave them a *V*-for-victory sign.

"Excuse me, sir," the guard said, clearing his throat.

The man turned around, smiling pleasantly. "Yes? Is there a problem, officer?"

"Well, Mr.—uh—" the guard stammered.

"Mr. Doyle," the man said politely.

The guard pointed to the Snoopers. "Mr. Doyle, these kids seem to think you had something to do with the jewelry-store robbery we had here a little while ago."

Mr. Doyle blinked in surprise. "Why would they think that?" he asked.

"They said a man with curly white hair was in—" the guard began.

"Maybe it was Santa Claus," Mr. Doyle interrupted. He laughed at his joke.

"It was *not* Santa Claus," Jessica said angrily. "It was you. I saw you and the other man in Mr. Fox's store."

"You must be confusing me with someone else, little girl," Mr. Doyle said. He was smiling, but his eyes were far from friendly.

"I hope you don't mind my asking," the guard said. "But what are you doing in the mall today, Mr. Doyle?"

"A little Christmas shopping for my family," Mr. Doyle explained patiently. "That's not against the law, is it?"

"No, sir. Sorry to bother you." The guard was red with embarrassment. He looked at the Snoopers. "OK. You heard what the man said."

"But he's lying!" Jessica said hotly.

"That's enough," the guard replied. "Don't make any more trouble, or else I'll have your parents take you home."

"Oh, don't scold them too much," Mr. Doyle said cheerfully. "It's the season to overlook little mistakes."

"That's very generous and kind of you, Mr. Doyle. I'm really sorry to have bothered you. Enjoy your shopping." The guard turned and walked away.

Instantly Mr. Doyle's friendly smile disappeared. He gave the Snoopers a steely glare. "You kids, beat it," he growled. "Keep out of my way, or *you'll be sorry.*"

CHAPTER 7

The Chase Is On

Elizabeth held her breath as Mr. Doyle walked away. Then she let out a loud sigh.

"Now he knows we know," Eva whispered, her eyes wide.

"What should we do?"

"It's a race to find the diamonds," Todd said with grin of pure excitement.

Elizabeth noticed a clock nearby. "It's also a race against time," she reminded them. "We only have forty-five minutes to go."

"Oh, no!" Ellen wailed. "Where should we start?"

"We can't let Mr. Doyle get the diamonds," Jessica said. "I think we should follow him. That way, if he finds them, we'll be there to stop him."

Elizabeth nodded. "OK. He just got on the up escalator."

"Yikes!" Amy said. "Let's go!"

The Snoopers ran through the crowd to the escalator, dodging past men carrying shopping bags, and ladies pushing strollers, and teenagers walking hand in hand.

"Excuse me, pardon me," Elizabeth mumbled.

Up ahead they could see Mr. Doyle's white head as he rode up to the second level. "He's going back to the scene of the crime!" Todd called out in a loud voice.

Several people turned to stare, including Mr. Doyle. When he reached the top of the escalator, he turned to the left, away from Mr. Fox's store.

"He's trying to trick us," Lila said. "But we're trickier than he is."

Elizabeth saw another clock as they jumped off the escalator onto the second-floor court. "We're running out of time," she said nervously.

"Come on, don't let him get away," Winston said.

The Snoopers hurried after him, trying not to attract attention. The moment Mr. Doyle stopped and gazed in the window of a stationery store, the Snoopers came to a sudden halt. Eva bumped into Ellen, who stumbled into Winston and Amy, who stepped on Lila's feet, who jumped backward into Todd and Jessica and Elizabeth.

"Shh!"

"Be careful!"

"Watch out!" they muttered to one another nervously. Elizabeth and the other Snoopers gazed into the store window in front of them with steady concentration. They were all looking at a pyramid-shaped stack of soap as though it were the most fascinating thing in the mall.

Then Mr. Doyle continued strolling along, and the Snoopers sped after him.

"He knows we're tailing him," Ellen said in a quivering voice. "What if he starts to chase us?"

"He won't," Winston said.

But Winston spoke too soon. Mr. Doyle turned around abruptly and headed their way. Jessica instantly clapped both hands over her mouth.

The Snoopers and Mr. Doyle stared

at one another. Mr. Doyle didn't say anything. He just scowled at them, and then crossed the aisle and went into a department store. After a moment the detectives began to follow.

"Wait a second." Elizabeth stopped, and the other Snoopers looked back at her in surprise.

"He's getting away, Liz," Jessica warned. "We can't take a rest."

"What if he just walks around and around, trying to trick us?" Elizabeth asked. "He might do that for a whole hour, and we won't have a chance to find the diamonds. We're wasting time following him."

"But we have to make sure he doesn't find them, either," Jessica said.

"Let's split up," Todd suggested. "Half of us follow him, half of us look for the diamonds."

"Perfect," Elizabeth said. "Some of us can start at Mr. Fox's store and check every single hiding place until we get to the Christmas tree where Mr. Doyle's partner was caught."

"OK, OK!" Jessica said. "But if we don't want to lose Mr. Doyle, we have to go now. He's getting away!"

CHAPTER 8

Time for Action

Jessica, Eva, Ellen, and Winston went into the department store. The air was filled with perfume from the cosmetics counters. Two women in white smocks were strolling among the crowd, spraying more perfume into the air. Jessica got spritzed in the face and began to sneeze.

"Where—*achoo!*—did Mr.—*achooo!*—Doyle go?" she asked.

Winston crouched behind a mannequin wearing a lacy nightgown and peeked around it to search the area.

"He's over there, looking at scarves," he hissed.

They watched in nervous silence as Mr. Doyle made a few purchases. Jessica saw some watches in a display case nearby. It was three forty. They had only twenty minutes left. She tried on a pair of dark glasses, always keeping Mr. Doyle in sight.

"How do we make sure he doesn't run into the other group?" Ellen whispered. She was trying on sunglasses, too. "They need time to find the diamonds without him getting in the way."

Winston tiptoed over and put on a pair of sunglasses with orange frames. Eva slipped on a pair shaped like cats' eyes. The four of them stood at the counter, keeping a lookout for the diamond thief from behind their disguises.

"We need some way to keep him busy," Jessica said.

"He's coming this way!" Winston warned. "He's leaving."

"Time for action," Eva said. She slipped off her sunglasses and stepped right in front of Mr. Doyle.

"That's my bag!" Eva shouted.

Mr. Doyle stopped in his tracks. "Beat it," he growled, his eyebrows drawn tightly together.

Eva took hold of his shopping bag with both hands. "That's my bag! He has my mommy's Christmas present!"

The perfume women came over, and several shoppers turned to look. Eva began to cry.

"He took my bag!" she wailed.

"It's a mistake," Mr. Doyle explained loudly as a crowd gathered. "You made a mistake, little girl. This is *my* bag."

"What's the problem?" asked the manager, hurrying over.

"He took my mommy's present. I spent all my money on it!" Eva sobbed and began stamping her feet. "Give it back!"

"Did you take this girl's bag?" the manager asked Mr. Doyle sternly.

Mr. Doyle was pink with anger. "I did not! She's just trying to make trouble!"

"Maybe someone should look in the bag," a teenage girl suggested. "Then we'll know for sure."

Mr. Doyle gritted his teeth and smiled, although Jessica could tell he was furious with them. He must have guessed that they were trying to sabotage his search for the diamonds.

"Go right ahead," he said to the manager.

The manager opened the bag and pulled out two silky scarves. "Is this what you got your mommy?" he asked Eva.

Eva gulped and glanced back at Jessica, Ellen, and Winston. "Ummm—I made a mistake," she whispered. "Sorry."

"You be sure of yourself before you create any more scenes, young lady," one of the perfume sprayers said.

"I will," Eva promised.

The crowd broke up, leaving the Snoopers and Mr. Doyle alone. "I warned you," the man said in a fierce tone. He shifted his raincoat to his other arm, and his car keys fell out of his pocket.

In a flash Jessica bent down and grabbed them.

"Run!" Winston yelled. "He can't get away without his car!"

"Hey! Give me my keys!" Mr. Doyle shouted.

At the same moment, Ellen stamped

on Mr. Doyle's foot. Eva knocked his shopping bag out of his hand, and Winston began waving his hands wildly in front of Mr. Doyle's face.

Jessica turned and raced out of the store.

CHAPTER 9

Got You

Elizabeth, Todd, Amy, and Lila stood outside Mr. Fox's jewelry store. They were busy scanning the area.

"Where could you hide a bunch of diamonds?" Todd asked.

"They were in a pouch," Elizabeth told them. "A black velvet pouch."

"Let's start looking," Lila said, inspecting a potted tree. Amy examined a display of mail-order cheese-and-sausage gift packs, and Todd checked underneath the benches, crawling on his hands and knees.

The railings of the balcony that over-looked the first floor were wrapped in evergreen garlands. Elizabeth began inspecting the fake-fir boughs. "Not here," she muttered.

Todd suddenly froze. "Look!" he gasped.

Ten feet away a janitor was emptying a trash can. Elizabeth felt a jolt like lightning zip through her. "Stop!" she yelled, running toward the janitor.

Startled, the custodian stepped back as Elizabeth and her friends began to ransack the garbage can, flinging aside empty soda cups and gum wrappers and ice cream–stained napkins.

"They could be in here!" Todd ex-claimed.

"I hope you kids have a good expla-nation for this mess," the janitor said.

They didn't answer. When Elizabeth

reached the bottom of the trash can, there was nothing left but a paper straw. "It's not here," she said. Then she looked up and noticed the janitor glowering at them.

"Oh, um, I thought I threw away my money," Lila explained, returning the garbage to the can.

The Snoopers replaced the trash as quickly as they could and hurried toward the escalator. From the top Elizabeth could see the clock over Santa's Village.

"We only have fifteen minutes left!" she announced.

"Where else can we look?" Amy moaned. "We looked in all the places the diamonds could be, up here."

"The first thief went through Santa's Village," Todd reminded them. "We have to look there. Come on."

"Excuse me, pardon me," Elizabeth mumbled as they hurried down the escalator. The Snoopers hit the ground, running, and rushed over to Santa's Village.

The line for photos with Santa stretched all the way to the food court. The Christmas carols and jingle-bell sounds were coming from a loudspeaker right over the line, and people were talking loudly over the noise. Two little boys were zooming around, pretending to be airplanes.

"Excuse me!" Lila said in a bossy voice as she tried to cut the line.

"You'll have to wait your turn like everyone else," an angry mother scolded. "That's not a nice way to behave at all."

Elizabeth felt her cheeks turn pink. "Sorry, but we have to get in there. It's important."

"If everyone acted that way, this place

would be a madhouse," an impatient father with a screaming baby said.

"You don't understand," Todd said.

"Where are your manners, young man?"

"Wait your turn like the rest of us!"

All around them, people were complaining about the endless line, about people who tried to cut in, and about how long everything was taking.

"How are we going to get in the Village?" Amy muttered.

Then another noise broke in through the Christmas carols.

Someone upstairs was yelling.

"Stop that girl!" a man shouted.

Elizabeth spun around. Jessica was racing down the escalator, with Mr. Doyle in pursuit, and Winston, Eva, and Ellen running after him. Jessica looked frantic.

"This way!" Lila shouted, yanking Elizabeth's arm.

They made for a gate in the Santa's Village fence that said, Elves Only. Jessica saw Elizabeth and Lila and made a beeline for them.

Mr. Doyle was almost close enough to catch her. But just then a noisy gang of high-school students crossed his path, and he was stuck.

"Move!" he shouted.

The teenagers swept him along like a boat on a river as Eva, Ellen, and Winston sprinted around them toward Santa's Village.

"Hurry!" Todd beckoned toward the backdoor of Santa's workshop. All the Snoopers burst inside, and Elizabeth was immediately tangled up in several elf costumes hanging on a rack.

"Help!" she called, trying to free herself.

"The diamonds have to be around here somewhere," Todd said. "There's nowhere else they could be."

"We'll split up," Eva said, panting. "We'll find them."

"I don't think so," a loud, booming voice broke in. "Now I've got you!"

CHAPTER 10

Santa and the Eight Elves

Jessica whirled around. Facing them from the opposite doorway was Santa Claus. For a moment no one spoke.

Then Jessica snapped out of it. "We're the new elves," she blurted out, grabbing an elf hat from the floor.

Santa Claus let out a laugh. "I thought so. You kids sure are late, though. I guess it took your parents some time to fill out all the forms in the mall office. Things are pretty hectic." He laughed again. "Now, hurry up," Santa said. "Spit spot!"

"Yes, sir." The Snoopers all nodded, snatching bits and pieces of elf costumes from the racks.

Ellen sat on the floor, tugging on a pair of pointy shoes with bells on the ends. Amy stuck a wig with a beard attached to it on her head, and Todd began buckling a three-inch-wide belt around his waist. Underneath the rack, almost hidden from view, Elizabeth sat, trying to untangle a button that had become snarled in her hair when she fell in among the costumes.

"Let's make it snappy, now, elves," Santa continued in a loud, jolly voice. "One, two, put on your shoe, three, four, there's the door."

"Hurry up," Jessica muttered to the others. "We have to get out there and start looking for—"

The backdoor suddenly flew open, and

Mr. Doyle stepped in. "Not so fast!" he said.

Jessica nearly jumped out of her skin. The thief's car keys jangled in her hand. Elizabeth ducked out of sight under the clothes rack.

"Santa, these kids are not signed up to be elves," Mr. Doyle said.

"Yes, we are!" Todd said quickly.

"No, they aren't," Mr. Doyle insisted through clenched teeth.

Santa Claus scratched his chin through his curly white beard. "They're not? Why do they say they are?"

"They're just trying to play a joke on me," Mr. Doyle said, glaring at Jessica. "Now, honey, give me back my car keys."

"Is this your granddaughter?" Santa asked in a puzzled voice.

"Yes," Mr. Doyle said.

"No," Jessica shouted.

Mr. Doyle chuckled. "Okay, joke's over, honey. You and your buddies have had your fun. Now we have to go."

Jessica grabbed Santa's hand. "He's not my grandfather," she said. "Honest, Santa, you have to believe me."

"He's not," Lila added. "He's a mean old robber."

"That's right!"

"He's not Jessica's grandfather!" The other Snoopers all chimed in at once, everyone yelling and trying to be heard.

"Quiet!" Santa called out.

Santa Claus stared at Mr. Doyle. Mr. Doyle stared at Santa Claus. Jessica squeezed Santa's hand. "You've got to believe me," she whispered. "Please let us go."

"I'm not sure what's what and who's who," Santa Claus said slowly. "Maybe

we should all go outside and straighten this out."

"No!" Jessica gasped as Santa pointed to the backdoor.

"Yes," Todd said, nudging Jessica with his hand. "We have a case to solve." He glanced nervously at Mr. Doyle.

Santa frowned. "Case? What case?" he asked.

Jessica gulped. "Nothing."

From under the costumes, Elizabeth peeked out and caught Jessica's eye. Nobody else noticed her. Elizabeth placed one finger over her lips and shook her head. Then she disappeared again.

"Okay," Jessica said. "We'll go."

CHAPTER 11

Rudolph

The moment the door closed, Elizabeth scrambled out from under the costumes. Any minute now Mr. Doyle would realize there was one nosy, snooping, troublemaking kid missing. Her. Elizabeth.

And the hour was nearly up.

"Where could they be?" she whispered out loud, glancing quickly around at the shelves and piles of costumes. "Where could you hide a whole bunch of diamonds? Think, Liz. Think!"

If the diamonds were still in the black

velvet pouch, they might be among the costumes. She began tossing hats and tunics and shoes all around the dressing room, frantically searching for the pouch. Jingling elf bells tinkled as she dug among the clothes, and spangling sequins flickered in the light. But there was no sign of the pouch or the diamonds. After a moment Elizabeth stopped, closed her eyes, and tried to concentrate.

"How could one diamond end up loose on the floor where we found it?" she wondered. "If the diamonds were all in the pouch, how could just one of them get out?"

Elizabeth bit her lip. She felt her heartbeat racing inside her. She had to figure it out. She just had to! With growing panic, she ran to the door and opened it to peek out at Santa's Village.

Drifts of fake snow lay here and there, ice crystals glittered along the fence, make-believe icicles hung from the workshop roof, and ice sculptures of toadstools and swans and dolphins sparkled brilliantly. Everywhere Elizabeth looked, there was ice.

"Ice," Elizabeth murmured to herself. She frowned. Something was nagging at the back of her mind. "Ice! Diamonds are called ice!"

That was it. The diamonds had to be lying out there in plain sight—disguised as ice. But where?

Elizabeth slipped through the door. Santa was sitting on his chair, his back to her. Several people waiting on line looked at her curiously, but she paid no attention to them. She had a million dollars' worth of diamonds on her mind.

Then she saw the clock. Elizabeth's

stomach swooped. There was one minute left! Without thinking, Elizabeth began zigzagging through Santa's Village, grabbing handfuls of fake snow everywhere she stopped. There wasn't a moment to lose. Her heart was racing, and her breath was coming in short gasps. In front of her was a bushy Christmas tree, and beside it, almost hidden from view, was a make-believe reindeer with a glowing red nose. "Rudolph!" Elizabeth whispered.

On Rudolph's brown, furry head, right between his antlers, was a cluster of glittering ice crystals. Elizabeth stared at Rudolph. His nose lit up.

Then Elizabeth held her breath and reached out her hand. The ice crystals were as hard as rocks and flashed as though filled with fire inside. "Found them," Elizabeth said as she scooped

up the diamonds in one hand.

At that precise moment Mr. Doyle stepped out from behind the Christmas tree.

"Thank you very much!" he said with a smile. "Now, hand them over to me."

CHAPTER 12

Ho, Ho, Ho!

Jessica turned frantically this way and that, trying to find Elizabeth in the crowd. Lila was tugging on her arm.

"Your father's coming!" Lila warned.

"We have to find Elizabeth," Jessica said urgently. She saw her father approaching through the crowd of shoppers. "Mr. Doyle disappeared," she added. "Liz could be in danger. He might even—"

"There!" Todd yelled, pointing across Santa's Village.

Jessica saw Elizabeth and Mr. Doyle half-hidden behind a Christmas tree.

Elizabeth was staring at Mr. Doyle with wide eyes. It looked as if one of her hands were filled with glittering ice. Mr. Doyle took a step toward her.

"Diamonds!" Jessica screamed as loudly as she could. "Liz found the diamonds!"

"Jessica!" Mr. Wakefield shouted, beginning to run.

Sixteen or seventeen different things began to happen all at once. Elizabeth shouted and ducked out of Mr. Doyle's reach, Mr. Wakefield jumped over the fence into Santa's Village, the security guards came running from all directions, Santa sprang out of his snow-covered throne, and Mr. Doyle made a break for it.

"He's getting away!" Eva shouted.

Santa Claus dove for Mr. Doyle and tackled him into a fake snowdrift just as the security guards surrounded them.

"Freeze!" a guard said.

Mr. Doyle lifted his head. His face was covered with snow. "Very funny," he snarled.

"Ho, ho, ho," Santa Claus said, sitting on Mr. Doyle's legs.

Mr. Wakefield ran to Elizabeth and caught her in his arms. "Are you all right?" he asked. "What's happening?"

"I found the diamonds, Dad!" Elizabeth said. "We all did. We knew they had to be around here, and we found them by ourselves."

Jessica climbed over the fence, and the other Snoopers followed. They surrounded Elizabeth.

"Wow, look at those diamonds!" Winston exclaimed. "I bet they're worth millions!"

A voice came to them through the

noise and hubbub. "Did someone find them?" Mr. Fox called out. "Did someone find my diamonds?"

The crowd parted, and Mr. Fox walked through the fake snow and ice to where the Snoopers were standing with Mr. Wakefield. Mr. Fox looked hopeful, but nervous too.

"Did someone really find them?" he asked a third time.

"Sure did," Elizabeth said, holding out her hand. "Look!"

The four diamonds flashed and sparkled as they moved in her palm. Mr. Fox let out a gasp of relief.

"I don't believe it. This is incredible," he said, turning to face the Snoopers. "You kids did this?" he asked in wonderment.

"That's right," Jessica replied proudly. She nudged Lila, who took the extra dia-

mond from her pocket and handed it to Mr. Fox.

"They're all here. This calls for a little celebration," Mr. Fox said with a tremendous smile. "And I think I know eight young detectives who deserve a reward."

"Seriously?" Todd asked. "This will be our first."

"Can we pick out *anything* in your store?" Lila asked with an eager sparkle in her eyes.

Mr. Fox laughed. "I have some beautiful crystal snowflake ornaments, and you may each have one," he said as he shook each Snooper's hand in congratulations. "And every time you look at them, I hope they remind you of these beautiful diamonds."

Elizabeth looked at Jessica and giggled. "You know what?" she said.

Jessica smiled. "What?"

"The wish I asked Santa Claus for came true."

From somewhere far away, through the crowded, busy mall, came a triumphant, "Ho, ho, ho!"

SIGN UP FOR THE SWEET VALLEY HIGH® FAN CLUB!

Hey, girls! Get all the gossip on Sweet Valley High's® most popular teenagers when you join our fantastic Fan Club! As a member, you'll get all of this really cool stuff:

- Membership Card with your own personal Fan Club ID number
- A Sweet Valley High® Secret Treasure Box
- Sweet Valley High® Stationery
- Official Fan Club Pencil (for secret note writing!)
- Three Bookmarks
- A "Members Only" Door Hanger
- Two Skeins of J. & P. Coats® Embroidery Floss with flower barrette instruction leaflet
- Two editions of *The Oracle* newsletter
- Plus exclusive Sweet Valley High® product offers, special savings, contests, and much more!

Be the first to find out what Jessica & Elizabeth Wakefield are up to by joining the Sweet Valley High® Fan Club for the one-year membership fee of only $6.25 each for U.S. residents, $8.25 for Canadian residents (U.S. currency). Includes shipping & handling.

Send a check or money order (do not send cash) made payable to "Sweet Valley High® Fan Club" along with this form to:

SWEET VALLEY HIGH® FAN CLUB, BOX 3919-B, SCHAUMBURG, IL 60168-3919

NAME _____
(Please print clearly)

ADDRESS _____

CITY_____ STATE _____ ZIP_____
(Required)

AGE _____ BIRTHDAY_____ /_____ /_____

Offer good while supplies last. Allow 6-8 weeks after check clearance for delivery. Addresses without ZIP codes cannot be honored. Offer good in USA & Canada only. Void where prohibited by law.
©1993 by Francine Pascal   LCI-1383-123

☎
1 (800) I LUV BKS!

If you'd like to hear more about your
favorite young adult novels and writers . . .
OR
If you'd like to tell us what you thought
of this book or other books
you've recently read . . .

CALL US at 1(800) I LUV BKS
[1(800) 458-8257]
Monday to Friday, 9AM – 8PM EST

You'll hear a new message about books and
other interesting subjects each month.

**The call is free, but please get
your parents' permission first.**